Abominable

An Aurora Bo Adventure

For our own little adventurers, Beatrix-Belle, Zachary and Elsa.
Stay curious little ones.

For our wonderful families and lovely men.

And for Lynne and Michael who faced life's final adventure.
We will love, miss and cherish you always.

Once upon a winter,
in a country made of snow,

there lived a little girl, and her name was **Aurora-Bo**.

A cheeky girl Aurora was,
one with a wicked grin.
She caused her parents worry,
with the **trouble** she'd get in.

Taking off at sunrise, on adventures who knows where,
it seemed that little Aurora, just didn't have a care.

On one especially snowy, cold and chilly day,
she left her house at sunrise, and set off on her way.

She trekked through snow so deep,

it reached up to her tummy,

with not one thought at all,

for her poor worried mummy.

After lots of walking,

she came upon a cave,

it looked so dark and scary,

she thought "I must be brave!"

She crept up to the opening,

and shouted out "Hello!"

But all that carried back to her,

was her own...

echo...

She shuffled further bit by bit,

until she stood inside,

and looking with her wicked grin,

thought

"What a place to hide!"

It was then she heard a rustle, followed by a **parp**,

and the biggest thing she'd ever seen **loomed** out of the dark!

MOSTLY EYES
GAPING MOUTH
COVERED IN HAIR
WHITE AS SNOW
GREAT BIG SIZE

EYES

GAPING
MOUTH

HAIR HAIR

GREAT

BIG

SIZE

WHITE
AS
SNOW

Its head was mostly eyes, with a gaping mouth below,

all covered head to toe in hair, which was as white as snow.

Despite its great big size, and covering of hair,

Aurora felt she knew for sure, this wasn't just a bear.

Aurora could remember,

she had seen this face before,

it was in her "**Big Book of Beasts**,"

of this she could be sure.

She tried her best to picture,

how the book began,

it was with the letter "A"

for

ABOMINABLE SNOWMAN!

Putrid Plants and Festering Funghi
By G.Rene Finger

Bumble Bees Rule the World

The Grape Escape & The Late Lemon

Bare Bum Boo & The Naked Escaper

Milly and Molly and Billy and Bob

Once Upon a Midnight   by Cindy Rella

Wild Woodland Wandering by Ava Stroll

A Bear Unaware— Izzy Grizzly

Inside the Witches Mind by Ron Cauld

HOW TO FIGHT VAMPIRES by Holly Stake

Invisible creatures and where to find them
By Luke Harder

The purple fish with a Christmas Wish!
P.H. Dawes

A Is for

Abominable

Beware this frightful creature
Of the caves and mountains.
Very dangerous
and terrible in every way

Page 72

Page 73

"You're the Abominable Snowman!"

Aurora screamed and shook,
while the creature just stood there, with a very puzzled look.
He pulled his mouth to the side, then scratched his great big head,

Aurora took a breath,
and stopped her
great big bellow,

and thinking hard replied,

"I'm not sure I really know..."

"I think we should find out immediately!"

Aurora loudly announced,

"We should check it at once in my book,
its back home at my house!"

With a nod and a wicked grin,
Aurora grabbed the beast,
who thought it best to go along...

...just to keep
the peace.

She dragged the creature by the hand, through the snow and wood,

the creature thought to argue now would not do any good.

And so they kept on trudging, the most peculiar pair,

the little girl, a wicked grin, and the creature covered in hair.

After they had walked a while,
they came to Aurora's house.

"Now,
you wait
here creature,

be as quiet
as a mouse!"

"Sit here on this swing set, and wait for my return,
I'll get my book, we'll look it up, about you we will learn!"
The creature sat down softly, just like she had said,
and visions of his lovely cave filled his hairy head.

Aurora leapt from the house,

her book held high in the air,

"I have it here for you creature,

I don't think it's very fair!

It says here you are **abominable**,

a most **hateful** creature indeed,

I don't agree in the slightest,

it's not at all what I see."

"So from this, I conclude, it is not you,

and using my brain as I can,

have decided you are not **abominable**,

you are just a **normal** snowman!"

With a nod and a wicked grin,
the creature was pulled to his feet,
a pipe and a carrot
were shoved in his face
and a hat on his head
nice and neat.

"Much better." Aurora said,

Big
Book of
Beasts

(feeling proud of herself,)

and grinning, went back in the house,
and returned the book to its shelf.

The creature stood there 'til nightfall,
with his carrot, hat and pipe,
and missing his cave and his dinner,
felt his tummy start to gripe.

With two quick glances around him, one to his left and his right,
he yanked off the hat, pipe and carrot, and fled off into the night.

The very next morning at sunrise,

Aurora looked out her window,

and seeing the hat pipe and carrot,

assumed he had turned back to snow.

The creature, it moved from the cave,

to somewhere much further away,

and lives there,

happy,

alone,

and child free...

...to this very day.

32025947R00023

Printed in Poland
by Amazon Fulfillment
Poland Sp. z o.o., Wrocław